✦ A Note about the Story ✦

This story is loosely based on the British tale "The King of Colchester's Daughters" (also known as "The Three Heads in the Well"). A version of the original can be found in *The Classic Fairy Tales* by Iona and Peter Opie; an abridged form is in *Folk-tales of the British Isles* by Kevin Crossley-Holland.

The Opies note that the story was already traditional by Elizabethan times. A version of the story was included in George Peele's play *The Old Wives Tale,* dated 1595, which provided added incidents and details.

I also consulted parallel tales, including the title story in Norah and William Montgomerie's *The Well at the World's End: Folk Tales of Scotland;* the story "Jack and the Water Fae the World's End" in Duncan and Linda Williamson's *Folktales of the Scottish Traveling People;* and a tale by Norwegian folklorist Jorgen Moe entitled "Bushy Bride" that is included in Andrew Lang's *The Red Fairy Book.*

For my nieces Andrea, Yvette, Noelle and Michelle,
who embody the very best of Princess Rosamond —R. S.

To my grandmother, Sherry Walsh —R. W.

Text © 2004 by Robert D. San Souci.
Illustrations © 2004 by Rebecca Walsh.
All rights reserved.

Type design by Sara Gillingham.
Typeset in Baskerville Book and Jot.
The illustrations in this book were rendered in a mixture of acrylic and watercolor.
Manufactured in China.
ISBN 1-58717-212-7

Library of Congress Cataloging-in-Publication Data is available.

Distributed in Canada by Raincoast Books
9050 Shaughnessy Street
Vancouver, British Columbia V6P 6E5

10 9 8 7 6 5 4 3 2

Chronicle Books LLC
85 Second Street
San Francisco, California 94105

www.chroniclekids.com

The Well at the End of the World

By Robert D. San Souci ❖ Illustrated by Rebecca Walsh

chronicle books · san francisco

The King of Colchester

The King of Colchester was a kind and just man, but not a very good ruler. Oh, he did fine dubbing knights or deciding what to have for dinner. But it was his daughter, Princess Rosamond, who really ran the kingdom. She advised her father on matters of state, kept the royal accounts, and fixed the drawbridge when it wouldn't rise or lower.

People often said it was a shame she wasn't beautiful, too. But practical Rosamond would just laugh and say, "I prefer good books to good looks. I may not be pretty, but my father's treasury is in order, the drawbridge works, and I've almost saved up enough for a new set of royal dishes!" When they hinted she might never wed, she merely replied, "I've no interest in a suitor who can't look deeper than a dimple!"

The widowed king was lonely. So he wed the beautiful Lady Zantippa, whose daughter, Zenobia, was also pretty. Unfortunately, the two were pretty good schemers, and they had their eyes on the royal treasury. They quickly made trouble for Rosamond, nagging the king day and night.

"Your daughter hates me," the queen complained, pretending to weep while dabbing with a handkerchief at dry eyes. "And she is jealous of lovely Zenobia."

"It's true!" whined the deceitful daughter. "And I love her like a sister."

It broke Rosamond's heart to see her father so upset. To keep peace, she went to live with her aunt in a distant town.

In short order, Zantippa and Zenobia spent the treasury on jewels and clothing. Then they badgered the king to keep raising taxes until he protested, "My poor people have nothing left but cares and worries!"

"Then tax them on their cares," insisted Zantippa, trying on a feathered hat.

"With a surtax on their worries," added Zenobia, twirling in her new gown.

Worn out, the unhappy ruler fell ill. When he begged to see Rosamond, the queen lied and said, "Your cruel daughter refuses to come."

At this, the king slipped into a deep sleep from which no one could wake him.

Rosamond heard of her father's illness. She raced to his side, but she could not rouse him. Then a washerwoman whispered to her, "Water from the well at the end of the world could heal your father. But the way is long and dangerous."

"My only fear is for my father," said the princess, who prepared to leave at once.

When the queen refused her a carriage, Rosamond merely shrugged. "Feet were invented before wheels," she said, pulling on her sturdiest boots. Then with a pitcher to hold the healing water, she set off to find the wondrous well.

Hurrying across the courtyard, Rosamond collided with a regal gentleman, and they tumbled into the dust. As they brushed themselves off, the man introduced himself as Duke Ogbert—the uncle of Prince Egbert of distant Farnaway.

"Princess Rosamond—A pleasure to meet you," she said with a smile.

"My lady!" gasped the old man.

Seeing how he stared, Rosamond said with a chuckle, "Boots and a homespun dress— I may not look like a princess, but I assure you I am. At the start of a long journey, simple clothes and sturdy shoes are most practical. Forgive me, sir, but I must be on my way now!"

As she hurried off, Duke Ogbert thought, "Why, that gentle lady seems the perfect bride for my nephew. Egbert will have nothing to do with princesses like Vaingloria or Gilda, who judge themselves by a mirror and a prince by his treasury." So he sent a message to the Prince of Farnaway urging him to send an offer of marriage at once to the Princess of Colchester.

Rosamond walked for days. One morning, enjoying a simple breakfast, she saw a scruffy little man in front of a cave. He called out,

"Young woman, young woman, with bread and cheese,
Will you just give me a taste of these?"

"I'll gladly share what I have," said Rosamond. "Then I must go on to the well at the end of the world. Its water may save my father's life."

When they had finished, the little man handed Rosamond a small hickory wand, telling her,

"Where briars block the way for you,
Three taps with this will pass you through."

Rosamond thanked him and continued on her way.

Soon Rosamond came to a thorny hedge that stretched across
the horizon. She waved the wand, and a passage opened.
Beyond lay a meadow, where a sad-eyed pony was tied to a
tree. The creature was little more than skin and bones, and Rosamond's
heart went out to it. The pony called,
"Young woman, if you set me free,
I'll speed you over land and sea."

The moment Rosamond untied the rope, the little horse changed into a mighty unicorn with dazzling mane and silver hooves. "Climb up," he told Rosamond, "and tell me where you wish to go."

"To the well at the end of the world," she replied.

Away they flew to the end of the world, where Rosamond found the well.

But as Rosamond bent to dip her pitcher, she suddenly gasped and stepped back.
A golden head floated up, then a second, and a third. All three heads sang to her:

"Raise us to feel the sun and the breeze,

We long to gaze at the flowers and trees."

Rosamond gently set the heads on the rim of the well, where they chattered happily
for a while. Then they sang,

"Young woman, kind woman, we thank you with feeling!

Now please return us to the water of healing."

When Rosamond had set the golden heads afloat, the first sang,

"Each time you comb your hair you'll find,

Treasures as fine as the thoughts in your mind."

As this head sank from sight, the second sang,

"A lover intelligent, gentle, and true,

Will find his long sought-after soul mate in you."

When this one had gone, the last head sang,

"To the already promised true love and new wealth,

I promise this water will restore the king's health.

As the last head vanished, Rosamond absentmindedly smoothed her hair. Jewels, coins, and flowers rained down. Catching her reflection in the water, she saw she had also been gifted with an elegant new gown.

"Bless their hearts—or heads!" she exclaimed. "Just knowing my father will be cured is reward enough!" Then, putting aside any thoughts of riches or romance, she quickly filled her pitcher, remounted the unicorn, and sped back to Colchester.

When Rosamond arrived at the castle, Queen Zantippa and Princess Zenobia gaped at her as she explained that she had been given gifts of healing, riches, and (someday) true love from the well at the end of the world. But Zantippa refused to let Rosamond see the king; she was determined to become sole ruler of Colchester when the king died. Even when Rosamond offered her jewels and gold from her hair, Zantippa would not give in.

The queen pulled Zenobia aside and snarled, "How dare she? Now she's richer than you!"

"And her gown is more beautiful than any of mine," wailed her daughter. "She'll have first pick of the best princes."

"Go to the well at the end of the world," her mother commanded. "Find out how to become even richer and prettier than Rosamond."

Zenobia set out in the royal carriage filled with luggage and hampers of delicious food, with knights and servants accompanying her. By chance she paused to picnic near the cave of the ragged little man. He called out,

> "Young woman, young woman, I implore you,
> For just a taste of what's spread before you."

But Zenobia said nastily, "You shan't have a bite, you horrid little man!" Then she ordered her servants, "Pack up every scrap, leave nothing behind."

The man shook a thorny branch at her, saying,

> "You'll find a hedge grown thrice as thick,
> With painful briars that snag and stick."

Zenobia merely laughed at his warning and ordered her carriage on. When she came to the wall of briars, the carriage would not pass. But Zenobia thought of the wealth and beauty that awaited her and in she plunged. Thorns tore her skin and skirts, but with greed as her shield, she made it through.

In the meadow beyond, a skinny little horse tied to a tree called to her,

"*Young woman, if you will set me free,*
I'll speed you over land or sea."

Zenobia sneered, "I wouldn't be seen on such a sack of bones as you!"

Off she marched, choking on dust, bruising her feet on stones, dirt caking her fine gown and slippers.

At last, filthy and exhausted, Zenobia reached the well at the end of the world. Prying up rocks and poking her nose into clumps of weeds, she hunted furiously for signs of magic that promised gold and jewels. Finding not a glint of riches nor a hint of new beauty in her mirror, she grew angrier and angrier.

Then the three golden heads floated up and sang,

"Raise us to feel the sun and the breeze,
We long to gaze at the flowers and trees."

But cruel Zenobia thumped the heads, saying, "Take *that!* How dare you speak to me, you frightful things? I am a princess royal!"

At this, the first golden head sang,

> "Snag-toothed, long-nosed, sail-eared, cross-eyed,
> Ugliness matches your heart inside."

As this head sank, the second sang,

> "Your hair breeds frogs and newts and weeds,
> Mean as your thoughts of spite and greed."

When this one, too, had sunk, the third sang,

> "Swollen with pride in how you act,
> Your airs have puffed you up in fact."

"Rude creatures!" Zenobia sniffed. "I'd order their heads chopped off, if they had anything to be chopped off of!" Then she saw her reflection in the well. She was ugly as her sins. Grabbing her hair in dismay, she squeezed out frogs and newts and muddy weeds, for her scalp was now a swamp.

Horrified, Zenobia fled. But her pride had swollen her like a balloon—she kept floating up into the sky until she tied stones to her feet.

Zenobia was so repulsive that the hedge drew aside in disgust. Her servants, unable to bear the sight of her, returned her to the castle in record time.

Queen Zantippa screamed when she saw her. Then the two began weeping. But their tears stopped when a messenger arrived, saying that Prince Egbert of Farnaway wanted to marry "the Princess of Colchester."

"I have heard he is very rich and terribly handsome," said the queen, scheming again. She eyed Zenobia and added, "We'll just keep you covered until after the wedding."

That evening, the mother and heavily veiled daughter hurriedly left the castle in a curtained carriage, escorted by fifty knights.

With the queen away, Rosamond slipped into her father's chamber and gave him a sip of healing water. He awoke instantly. His joyful daughter explained about the wonderful well, and the king was moved by the love and courage she had shown reaching it. He was doubly delighted when Rosamond reported, "The queen and Princess Zenobia have disappeared on some mysterious errand."

"Then we'll have some peace and quiet!" the king rejoiced.

He soon felt well enough to meet with Duke Ogbert, who was astonished to see him in the company of Rosamond. "But I was told the Princess of Colchester had already left to wed my nephew, Prince Egbert, who had sent an offer of marriage," he said. "I plan to leave shortly to attend the wedding."

"Villains and vipers! Zantippa and Zenobia have gone to Farnaway to wed the prince to the wrong princess!" exclaimed Rosamond. "I'm not interested in marrying someone I haven't met, but I won't let them deceive him in my place." And off she ran to the royal stable.

At Queen Zantippa's insistence, the wedding had already begun. The prince, who had sneaked a look at his bride-to-be, entered the chapel with wobbly knees, but he was determined to keep his word.

Zenobia shuffled down the aisle in heavy lead slippers that kept her on the ground. She had just reached the prince's side when the chapel doors burst open. Rosamond entered, astride the unicorn.

"You must stop this wedding!" she cried to the prince. "Zenobia has tricked you. I am the Princess of Colchester your uncle intended."

"Liar!" screamed Zenobia.

"Scheming wretch!" screeched Zantippa.

But the unicorn said to the queen,

"Your daughter's no true princess bride,
Let Rosamond stand at the prince's side."

So saying, he kicked Zenobia hard enough to knock her out of her lead slippers, and she began to bounce around the church. When Zantippa tried to catch her, the queen's ringed fingers caught in the bridal veil. The two bounced together from altar to choir, over the heads of the astonished guests, and out the doors, never to be seen again.

When Rosamond's father and the prince's uncle arrived, they discovered the guests enjoying the wedding feast—even though there had been no wedding. Rosamond and Egbert laughed together as they told the story of the bouncing bride and her mother bounding into the distance. And Rosamond realized that Egbert, as well as having a sense of fun, was kind and wise and even-tempered—the very virtues he found so appealing in her.

They soon fell in love; and, in time, there was indeed a wedding. When he became king, Egbert proved no better at running a kingdom than Rosamond's father. So she wound up helping them both keep accounts balanced and drawbridges in working order.

And with the gold and jewels from her hair, Rosamond helped the needy in both kingdoms, and still had enough left over to buy her father a new set of royal dishes.

People would often say what a handsome couple she and Egbert made, but they found their true joy reading good books to each other by the fire every evening, sharing a good laugh, and simply enjoying the pleasure of each other's company.